First published 2004 by Walker Books Ltd
87 Vauxhall Walk, London SE11 5HJ

2 4 6 8 10 9 7 5 3

Book design by Fiona Andreanelli
based on artwork by Heinz Edelmann
Story adapted by Charlie Gardner from the screenplay
by Lee Minoff, Al Brodax, Jack Mendelsohn and Eric Segal
With thanks to Roger McGough

This book has been typeset in Futura and Amelia

Printed in China

British Library Cataloguing in
Publication Data: a catalogue record for
this book is available from the British Library

ISBN 0-7445-8652-6

www.walkerbooks.co.uk

THE BEATLES

Yellow Submarine

WALKER BOOKS
AND SUBSIDIARIES
LONDON · BOSTON · SYDNEY · AUCKLAND

Pepperland: 80,000 leagues beneath the sea it lay – or lies, I'm not too sure – a winterless wonderland where song and laughter rode on the breeze, and where you never felt lonely because **Sergeant Pepper's Band** was always playing your song.

But if, like the **Chief Blue Meanie**, you didn't have a song and you hated music, then you might have wanted to sneeze Pepperland away for ever.

The Chief inspected the Meanie Army. "Are my troops in readiness?"
"Ready, Your Blueness!" **Max** nodded furiously.
The troops stood to attention:

the **apple bonkers**,

the **snapping Turks**,

the four-headed **bulldogs**,

and the dreadful flying **Glove**.

"*Splendid!*" the Chief's big teeth gnashed. "Today, Pepperland goes blu-ey!"

Captain Fred ran for his life as the crowd scattered. "The Meanies are coming, the Meanies are coming!" Those who dared to stay were beaten blue and blue by the Glove or frozen like colourless statues.

The Chief Blue Meanie gloated. "If music be the food of Glove, play on!" And the air turned blue with his laughter.

Only Fred and the **Old Lord Mayor** escaped.

"Hurry, young Fred!" wheezed the Lord Mayor.

Eventually they reached the great grey pyramid that marked the edge of Pepperland. At the top a stubborn streak of ochre stained the sky: a **yellow submarine**.

"Our music is fading, young Fred," the Mayor began. "Pepperland is dying."

"But Lord Mayor, there must be something I can do!"

"There is," he whispered. "Climb aboard the submarine and get help. You're the only one of us left who can carry the tune…"

Fred climbed in and set sail.

Eight days and 80,000 leagues later, the yellow submarine surfaced in Liverpool.

In Hope Street, **Ringo** felt hope-less.

"Liverpool can be a lonely place on a Saturday night," he mused, "and this is only Thursday morning. Nothing ever happens to me!"

Like a goldfish in a murky puddle, the submarine followed him home.

Captain Fred hammered on the door. "Help! I really need somebody – Help!"

"Thanks, we don't need any," said Ringo.

"**H** for Hurry, **E** for *Er-gent*, **L** for Love Me Do and **P** for Please, pl-ea-se help me!" pleaded Fred.

Ringo creaked open the door. "Your story has touched my heart … come in."

"Bless you!"

"Did I sneeze?" Ringo smiled.

Ringo led Fred into a gallery.

"I'm sure we can work it out … with a little help from my friends."

They bumped into Frankenstein.

"Frankenstein's a friend of yours?" Fred said.

"Oh, yeah… I used to go out with his sister … Phyllis."

The monster unbolted itself into **John**. Then they found **George** and **Paul**.

"Hey, John! Hey, Paul! Hey, George!" called Ringo. "Listen to old Fred!"

"Music … Lord Mayor … submarine … explosions … Blue Meanies," he gabbled.

"What do you think?" said Ringo.

"I think," said John, "he needs a rehearsal."

Fred welcomed them aboard.
"Right then, let's get this
vessel shipshape!"
"I kinda like it the way
it is …" said John,
"…submarine shape."
"Do we need a ticket to
ride?" asked George.
"Only if we're taking the
mystery tour," Ringo joked.
"How d'ya start it?" Paul asked.
"With a key," said Ringo. "Give us an **'A'**, Paul!"

"Eh? Where's the handbrake then?"
"Perhaps this is it?" Ringo said.
"I'm a born lever-puller, me…"

The motors gurgled into
life. Then the propellers,
turning at a steady
33⅓ rpm, hummed
and drummed their
goodbye to Liverpool …

...and the little submarine dived deep below the waves.

Time stood still for a moment; the clocks were striking for shorter hours. They drifted into a monstrous sea – a **Sea of Monsters**.

John gazed out of a porthole. "There's a school of whales."

"They look a bit old for school…" George said.

"University, then … University of Wales!"

Teapots poured out their lonely hearts to the soulful sound of an ice-cream cornet.

Kinky-Boot Beasts danced and kicked the little submarine all around the seabed, until …

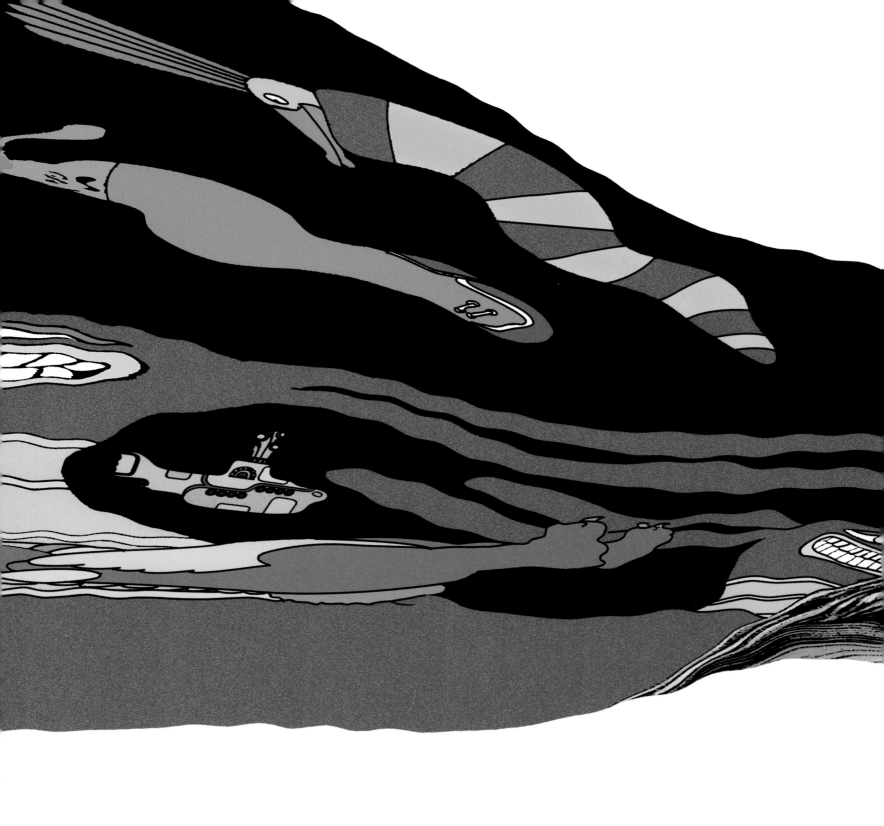

...a riptide sent them spiralling off course. It was the hideous **Suckophant**, hoovering everything in its path!

"It's the dreaded vacuum flask," said George. "What shall we do?"

"Have a nice cup of tea," John said. "So long, sucker!"

But they were gone – swallowed into his monstrous belly of oblivion...

It was an inside-outside world that greeted them: a nowhere land, empty save for a curious creature dancing and singing a jig with no tune.

"Ad hoc, ad loc and quid pro quo.
So little time, so much to know!"

George looked on. "He must be the **Nowhere Man**."
The little man passed Ringo a card:

Jeremy Hilary Boob, PhD
Eminent Classicist, Botanist, Satirist
Part-time Firefighter and Paperback Writer

"A real man of letters, eh?" Ringo smiled. "Why don't you come with us, Mr Boob?"
"You mean, you'd take a *nowhere man?*"
"Yeah. Come on, we'll take you somewhere."

"Where are we?" Paul asked. "It looks like a **Sea of Holes**!"

"Or a holy sea!" George quipped. "Where's the exit gone?"

"Let's get searching, fellas." Paul took charge.
"Look for a hole that says Way Out, man!"

"There's a hole in my pocket," Ringo puzzled.
"Maybe that's the way out?"

Only one hole led to
Pepperland, and
through it came
a Blue Meanie.
Jeremy had
been kidnapped!
"Hey, where's
the Booby gone?"
Ringo pined.

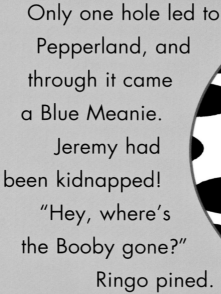

"Maybe he fell
into a booby trap?"
Paul joked.
"You mean
like this one?
Aaaaaaaaaaagh…"
And the others
followed Ringo,
plummeting into the darkness…

"**S**o this is Pepperland." John was unimpressed. "It's a bit dingy."

"It makes me want to sing the blues," said Paul.

"All right," said John, "let's *sing*!"

The Lord Mayor stirred. "Do I hear music? Do I see young Fred?" The old man's heart beat stronger with every bar. "And who are these familiar faces? You're the spitting image of Sergeant Pepper's Band – you could impersonate them and lead a rebellion!"

As the night crept in,
the lads, quiet as cats' paws, crept
out to Sergeant Pepper's bandstand,
picking a path between clumps of
snoring Blue Meanies.

"Look, I've found their uniforms!"
John whispered.

George was impressed. "Hey, nice
bit of gear that."

"Let's get some kip, fellas," Paul
yawned. "Tomorrow, we're going to
make those Meanies look teeny-weenie!"

They got dressed and set off just as day broke.

"Instruments at the ready?" asked John. *"One … two … three…"*

The brass sparkled and announced the opening bars of a familiar anthem: Sergeant Pepper's Lonely Hearts Club Band was back! And one by one the Pepperlanders returned to life and colour.

The Blue Meanies held their hands to their ears, and wailed and gnashed their terrible teeth.

"WHO is responsible for this?" screamed the Chief Blue Meanie. "Squash them! Crush them! *O-BLUE-TER-ATE* them!"

The dreadful Glove snarled into battle...

"All you need is LOVE ... Glove," said John.

Sergeant Pepper's Band changed the tune: *All You Need Is Love*
filled the air and made it sweet again.

"*Love, Love, Love,*" sang John, "*All you need is Love.*"

And the Glove, filled with glovey love and happiness, flew away.

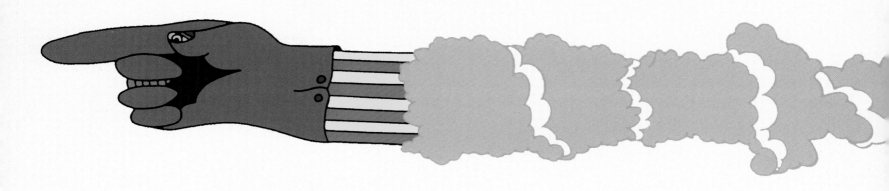

The Blue Meanies were on the run now, tumbling over the hills to the five corners of the earth. "You're attacking the wrong way!" raged their Chief. "Retreat … backwards!"

His four-headed bulldog headed in four
different directions. The war was over.
   "I'm going to blue-pencil you, *FOR EVER!*"
the great indigo puffball threatened Jeremy.

   "Peace, peace,
supplant the gloom,"
   Jeremy replied in verse.
   "Turn off what is sour,
turn into a flower,
and bloom, bloom,
BLOOM!"

   Spellbound, the
Chief Blue Meanie
was left in a rash
of rosebuds.
   "The first time I saw
that nobody," said Ringo
proudly, "I knew he was
a somebody!"

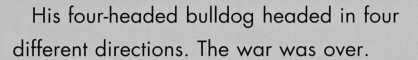

"Hello, blue people," John called. "Won't you join us?"
The Chief Blue Meanie wept huge blue tears.

"It's no longer a blue world, Max," he sobbed, his nose
flowering larger than ever.

"Maybe, Your *Bloomness*," smiled Max, "but the bluebird
of happiness will always be ours!"

"Are you with us?" John called again. "Why not mix,
hook-up, mingle?"

"What do you say … shall we mix, Max?"

"Oh YES, Your *Newness*!"

And for the first time in their existence, their mean,
unhappy lives became **happy** and **meaningful** because of
one simple phrase …